# Little
# HORRORS

## Shiver with fear...

Owwl!

## ...shake with laughter!

For Phyllis

Visit Shoo Rayner's website!
www.shoo-rayner.co.uk

ORCHARD BOOKS
96 Leonard Street, London EC2A 4XD
*Orchard Books Australia*
32/45-51 Huntley Street, Alexandria, NSW 2015
First published in Great Britain in 2003
First paperback edition 2003
Copyright © Shoo Rayner 2003
The right of Shoo Rayner to be identified as the author
and illustrator of this work has been asserted by him in
accordance with the Copyright, Designs, and Patents Act, 1988.
A CIP catalogue record for this book is available
from the British Library.
ISBN 1 84362 005 7 (hardback)
ISBN 1 84362 009 X (paperback)
1 3 5 7 9 10 8 6 4 2 (hardback)
1 3 5 7 9 10 8 6 4 2 (paperback)
Printed in Great Britain

# Little HORRORS

## The Snow Man

Shoo Rayner

ORCHARD BOOKS

An icy chill trickled down my back.

My sister Kim had got me in the neck with a freezing cold snowball!

"I'll get you!" I shouted.

"You'll have to catch me first!" she called as she tore down the hill, sliding on an old tin tray.

I chased after her, taking the short cut over the bump in the hillside.

Something moved at the bottom
of the hill. Kim was almost on top
of it when I realised what it was.

"Watch out, Kim!" I called. We dug our heels into the snow and slid to a halt in front of a woman and two huge white dogs.

She was dressed in white. Her eyes were icy blue. I felt her cold stare go right through me.

"What are you doing here?" Her words came out in thin icy wisps of breath.

We told her we were staying with our grandparents and pointed over at the house.

Her eyes narrowed. "That's Snowman's Cottage," she said. The dogs growled at the name, making me shiver.

"Haven't they told you about the
Snow Man?" she asked. "You've just
been sledging over him. He doesn't
like that... He'll try to come and get
in your house, mark my words!"

Then she tramped off with the
dogs and soon disappeared, melting
into the snow.

# We rushed back to the house.

"Who *is* the Snow Man?" Kim and I gasped, when we found Grandpa.

Grandpa opened his mouth to answer and the lights went out…

But it was only a power cut.

We had to light candles. It made the house look spooky. We told him about the strange lady we'd met that afternoon.

"That's Mrs Coldhart," Grandpa told us. "She's an old busybody."

Later, with firelight glittering in his eyes, Grandpa told us that there was a large white rock on the hill, just behind the house, that was shaped like a man.

"Long ago," he said. "On a stormy snowy night, a traveller knocked on the door of Snow Man's Cottage and asked to stay the night.

"The old lady in the cottage was frightened and wouldn't let him in."

"Legend has it that when the snow melted, the traveller had frozen into rock. His spirit poured flood water right into the house to pay the old woman back for being so unkind."

When Grandpa finished the story,
the house was silent. The fire cast
eerie shadows on the walls.

"D-d-d-do you think it's true, Grandpa?" I asked. "Do you think the Snow Man will try to get into the house like Mrs Coldhart said?"

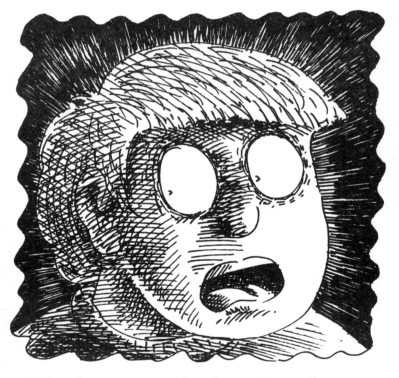

The house creaked as Grandpa whispered, "Who knows?"

The next day Kim and I climbed to the top of the hill and began building our own snowman. He was brilliant!

As we admired our handywork,
Mrs Coldhart tramped past. She
looked at our snowman and snorted.

"The Snow Man won't like that at
all," she said.

The dogs growled deeply.

Mrs Coldhart sniffed the air. "I hope you haven't upset the Snow Man. The weather is changing, so the snow will start melting tonight. That's when he'll try creeping into your house!"

Kim and I backed away from her and ran.

Granny was very cross when we told her what Mrs Coldhart had said.

"That interfering old woman!" she scowled. "She's got no business, scaring you like that."

"The Snow Man won't try to get in, will he, Grandpa?" Kim asked.

Grandpa smiled. "Don't you worry," he said, hugging us both. "The Snow Man is just an old piece of rock really."

In the middle of the night I woke up. The power had come back on and it was boiling hot.

I opened the steamed-up window.

From all around came the sound of dripping water.

Just a few last patches of snow
remained on the hill. One patch was
shaped like a-a-a...man!

I lay awake listening to the drip -
drip - drip of the melting snow. Was
the Snow Man trying to get in?

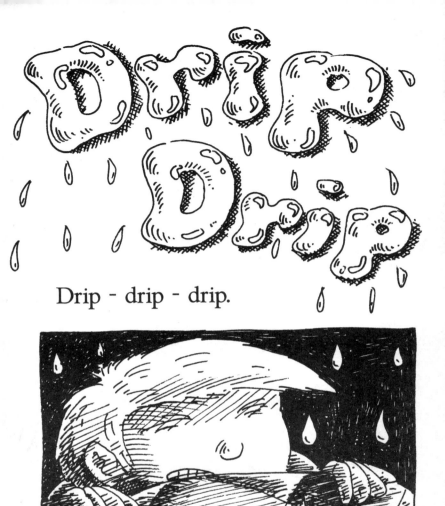

Drip - drip - drip.

I shut my eyes tightly. He couldn't get in…could he?

Drip - drip - drip…splash!

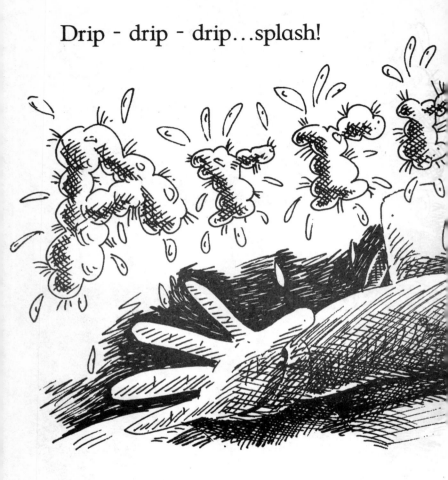

"Arrgh!" I yelled and jumped out of bed. A freezing blob of water had splashed on my face!

"The Snow Man's coming!" I
screamed.

Grandpa rushed in and switched the light on. It shone bright for a second, making wet sizzling noises.

Then it exploded, "BANG!"

Kim screamed in the doorway.

"He-e-e-lp! It's the Snow Man!"

"Quick!" said Grandpa, running down the stairs. "I'll turn the water off immediately!"

We heard him rummaging and
grunting under the kitchen sink as
he struggled to turn off the water
tap at the mains.

The water in my room slowed to a trickle, then to a drip before it finally stopped.

Peace settled on the house.

"Burst water pipe!" said Grandpa. "Nothing to do with the Snow Man. The pipes must have frozen in the attic and burst when the heating came on and the thaw set in."

The next day, we helped Grandpa to fix the burst pipe. I felt a bit silly that I'd believed Mrs Coldhart's story.

Later, Kim and I went to have a look at the Snow Man Rock. I felt he was watching us!

A stream sprang from his feet and tumbled down the hillside…

It swirled around our wellies, grabbing and pulling.

The water gurgled...
it seemed to be talking...
whispering...

"Let me in...let me in...let the
Snow Man in!"